Recess All-Stars

Don't miss the other Invincible Girls Club adventures!

Home Sweet Forever Home
Art with Heart
Back to Nature
Quilting a Legacy

THE INVINCIBLE GIRLS CLUB

BOOK 5

RECESS ALL-STARS

by Rachele Alpine

illustrated by Addy Rivera Sonda

Aladdin
New York   London   Toronto   Sydney   New Delhi

ALADDIN
An imprint of Simon & Schuster Children's Publishing Division
1230 Avenue of the Americas, New York, New York 10020
First Aladdin paperback edition November 2022
Text copyright © 2022 by Rachele Alpine
Illustrations copyright © 2022 by Addy Rivera Sonda
Also available in an Aladdin hardcover edition.
All rights reserved, including the right of reproduction in whole or in part in any form.
ALADDIN and related logo are registered trademarks of Simon & Schuster, Inc.
For information about special discounts for bulk purchases, please contact
Simon & Schuster Special Sales at 1-866-506-1949 or business@simonandschuster.com.
The Simon & Schuster Speakers Bureau can bring authors to your live event. For more
information or to book an event contact the Simon & Schuster Speakers Bureau
at 1-866-248-3049 or visit our website at www.simonspeakers.com.
Book designed by Heather Palisi and Ginny Kemmerer
The illustrations for this book were rendered digitally.
The text of this book was set in Celeste.
Manufactured in the United States of America 1022 OFF
2 4 6 8 10 9 7 5 3 1
Library of Congress Control Number 2021936036
ISBN 9781534475366 (hc)
ISBN 9781534475359 (pbk)
ISBN 9781534475373 (ebook)

To my neighborhood friends of West Point,
Valley Forge, and Germantown Drive;
thanks for a childhood spent playing endless games
of kickball in my front yard

In a perfect dream, things would be set exactly the way you would want them. But I think it's more interesting that in real life, things aren't exactly the way you planned.
–Naomi Osaka

Contents

STRIKING OUT

Today was the day.

I could feel it in my bones.

Well, I could feel it in my legs, which were aching from the nonstop pumping I'd been doing.

Today was the day one of my best friends, Myka, and I would go all the way over the top bar of the swing set on our playground.

Many at Erie Elementary had tried, but none had succeeded.

We were about to change that.

We were ready to go for the glory.

This was what the two of us had been preparing for, every day at recess.

"We've got this," Myka said, and grinned at me.

My feet kicked up little puffs of dirt as I gained momentum.

I gripped the chains so tight, it was as if someone had superglued my hands to them.

Higher and higher I went. I swear, my feet almost skimmed the bottom of the white cotton-candy clouds in the sky.

My best friends—in the Invincible Girls Club—had helped plan this moment out.

Emelyn, who loved science, had calculated how fast and high we'd have to go to make it over the bar, and Ruby had her camera ready to document it and planned to write an article about it for our elementary school newspaper.

"Are you ready for this?" I shouted to Myka.

"I was born ready!" she replied, and pumped even harder.

And I was too. Really, I was.

Well, okay, maybe I was a little teeny bit nervous.

Who wouldn't be? The swing set was massively tall, and I was about to catapult myself over it on a tiny piece of rubber and chains.

But what was life without a little adventure?

"Pump! Pump! Pump!" Ruby and Emelyn shouted from below.

"Higher! Higher! Higher!" Myka added in between their chants.

Other girls stood around clapping and bouncing from foot to foot as they waited to witness the event of a lifetime.

We had an entire cheering squad, and I refused to disappoint them.

One more pump, and I'd fly over the bar like a bird and come back down, the twisted chains around the top a memorial to our great feat.

Kids would talk about Myka and me for centuries.

We'd become local legends.

Teachers would include us in their history lessons.

The school would place a plaque next to the swing set to honor our accomplishments.

"Ready or not, here I go!" Myka yelled.

Emelyn and Ruby cheered louder.

All I had to do was go a little bit higher. Pump a little bit harder . . .

TWEEEEEEEEEEEEEEEEEEEEEEEEEEEEEEEET!

"Lauren and Myka, you slow down this instant!" a voice demanded. "You know the rules. You can't swing that high!"

I groaned.

Ms. Kratus.

The recess monitor.

Also known as . . . the destroyer of fun.

I was almost certain that if there was a good time to be had, Ms. Kratus could sniff it out and

stop it in its tracks. Every. Single. Time. She was never without her whistle, which she used for ultimate recess torture.

We couldn't throw snowballs in the winter, dodgeball had been banned, and once she had even tried to stop us from pretending that the ground was lava, as if we were running through actual lava. There was no doubt in my mind that if she could make it happen, she'd demand we take naps during recess.

"How many times do I have to tell you not to swing that high?" she demanded, and I was smart enough to know that was a question I wasn't supposed to answer.

I slowed down and jumped off the swing in midair.

TWEEEEEEEEEEEEEEEEEEEEEEEEEEEEEEET!

"No jumping off the swings!" she added as my dreams of becoming a playground legend were officially destroyed.

Myka slowed her swing down, got off, and followed me as I stomped over to our friends.

"It's so unfair! She never lets us have any fun," I said.

"I was totally about to go over," Myka added.

"What a bummer," Emelyn said.

"Don't worry," Ruby whispered. "You can try again in a few days when she's not looking."

"I'll be watching the two of you!" Ms. Kratus said, as if she could hear our conversation.

"Or maybe not," Ruby said, and frowned.

Myka gestured toward the field, where a big group of boys was playing kickball. "We should join them. Then we can have some fun."

"We should!" I said. "You're great at it when we play in gym class."

"Totally," she agreed, which was super modest because Myka was an amazing soccer player. I bet she'd be the best kickball player out there.

I watched the boys throw the ball and run around the bases.

Kickball.

Why hadn't I thought of playing with them before? Maybe our plan to go over the top of the swings had been destroyed, but we could be known for something else.

The kickball all-stars.

I liked the sound of that.

"Let's go!" I said, and gestured toward the rest of the Invincible Girls to come with me.

As we made our way toward the game, I watched Nelson at home plate. His foot connected right in the sweet part of the ball, and it sailed up into the air toward me.

"I've got it!" I yelled, and ran forward with my hands outstretched. The ball landed in my arms with a satisfying *thunk*, and I held it over my head like a prizefighter showing off her trophy. My friends cheered and congratulated me.

Except we appeared to be the only ones excited about the catch.

"Why did you do that?" Nelson demanded.

"Yeah! You cost us a potential win. Syed could have scored, and we would've been ahead," Brady complained.

I held the ball, not sure what to do.

Nelson came over and took it.

"I didn't mean to mess up your game," I told him. "I saw the ball coming and, well, I wanted to play."

"Play?" he asked.

"We all do," I said, and pointed toward my friends.

"Yep, we'll be great," Myka added. "I'm on the soccer team. Tell me where you want me to aim, and I should be able to get the ball right there!"

She pretended to kick a ball to show him that she had what it took.

"And I already proved to you that I could catch the ball," I said.

"This is *our* game and our field," Nelson said. "You girls have the playground."

Wait.

He didn't want us to play because we were *girls*?

"You're joking, right?" I asked. "Since when is the field only for boys?"

"It's always been our place," Nelson said.

"Um, why?" Ruby asked, joining the conversation.

"Because that's the way it is." Nelson turned his back to us and threw the ball to those waiting in the infield. "Okay, Brady, you're up!"

I made a face at Nelson's back and turned to my friends.

"This is ridiculous!" I said.

"You've got that right," Ruby agreed.

"Maybe the boys playing kickball is the way it has always been, but that most certainly isn't the way it will stay," I announced. "It's time to change that. It's time for a meeting of the Invincible Girls Club!"

YOU KICK LIKE A GIRL

I huffed and puffed all the way into the class-room, angry about not being able to play kickball.

Our teacher, Miss Taylor, asked, in a way-too-happy mood that didn't reflect the storm that was brewing in my mind, "How was lunch today?"

"Delicious!" Wesley said. "My dad packed me a piece of cake!"

"And I had leftover pizza!" Tyra said.

Lunch had been good. But recess. Recess had been a different story. I glared at the boys.

Miss Taylor sat at the edge of the desk with one leg crossed over the other. She bent toward us and spoke in a quiet voice, as if she had a secret to share.

"I have some exciting news for you," she announced.

We leaned forward, because she always had great things planned for us.

"This unit is one of my favorites of the school year. It's our career unit! We're going to learn about different kinds of jobs and explore something that you might be interested in! Including shadowing someone at their job!" She winked at us. "Not that you have to be just *one* thing when you grow up. You can be so many different things, and even do more than one at a time! Does anyone want to share what they might want to be?"

"How about a cake-decorating veterinarian who dances ballet?" Rhiannon asked.

"You would be very busy, but sure!" Miss Taylor replied.

"I'd be a great horse-riding painter," Tyra volunteered.

"That certainly would be interesting," Miss Taylor answered. "But maybe not at the same time!"

"Or a scuba-diving police officer," Mateo offered.

"Perhaps you can solve crimes underwater!" Miss Taylor told him, and we laughed. "You all have such great ideas. Why don't we take some time to brainstorm about the different jobs you can have? I bet you'll discover something you never thought of before."

"Did you discover teaching?" Ruby asked, always in news reporter mode.

Miss Taylor smiled. "Oh, no. Teaching was always something I wanted to do. I can't think of a time when I didn't want to be a teacher, but

I did discover that I really like art, too, which is why I make bracelets and sell them at craft fairs. That's part of the fun of this unit, to learn about and explore the options that are out there."

She grabbed a stack of paper and gave us each a sheet.

"What are we doing with these?" Mateo asked. He always asked questions before Miss Taylor had time to explain. If he'd wait five seconds more, he would have the answer.

"I want you to list as many jobs as you can come up with. No job is too silly or different. The idea is to help us discover jobs we might not have considered before. I'll give everyone ten minutes to put their ideas down."

"What are you going to write?" Emelyn asked me.

"Easy," I said, and bent over my paper. First I wrote *VETERINARIAN*, and then added *DOG WALKER* and *SPORTS BROADCASTER* in giant letters.

"The first two make sense," Ruby said. "But I didn't know you wanted to be a sports broadcaster! How cool!"

"Yes! You'd be a natural," Myka said. "You're great at calling games when we watch my brothers play. I might be into playing the sports, but Lauren knows everything you can about how they're played."

"You can thank Carter and Scott for that," I told them. "Family sports night has taught me a thing or two, and while I might not play football, I now love to watch it."

"Oh, I like that!" Ruby said. "You could broadcast all the games Myka competes in!"

"Yep, like when she's in the Olympics!" Emelyn added.

I grinned at them. I loved that my friends believed in me so much. I turned back to my sheet and added a few more ideas, other things that had to do with stuff that I loved, like a party planner, referee, and cupcake tester. When time was up, Miss Taylor asked us to stand and move around the room to check out each other's papers. "If you see an idea you like, go back to your seat and add it to your list."

It was fun to check out everyone's jobs, and before long the room was filled with the flurry of people talking.

"Kara! You'd make a great teacher!"

"A zookeeper? Now, that's cool!"

"I could totally see Mayra as a rock star!"

"A doughnut maker! That would be the tastiest job ever!"

We went from list to list commenting on everyone's choices, racing back to add more to our own. I was reading Emelyn's ideas when I heard a group of boys talking about the lists that the Invincible Girls had made. They laughed and pointed, so the four of us marched over to them.

"What's so funny?" Ruby asked with her hands on her hips.

"Your lists," Nelson said. "First you think you should have the kickball field, and now you think you can be a sports announcer?"

"Of course I can," I said.

"You don't even play football, so how in the world would you be able to call the game?"

If Nelson was trying to change our minds, it was definitely not working. When you were in a club whose goal was to prove how amazing girls can be, you *never* backed down from a challenge. I didn't even need to ask the other three if they felt the same way. I simply knew they did.

"Is that so?" I asked him. "Things are about to change. Because we're gonna prove you wrong. About our career unit *and* the kickball field."

Myka, Ruby, and Emelyn nodded in agreement.

I bent over my paper and in giant letters added one more career, perhaps the most important job there was.

INVINCIBLE GIRL.

BASE INVADERS

The thing about having the greatest friends in the world was that you never needed to ask for help; they just volunteered. Myka, Ruby, and Emelyn instantly agreed that this was our next assignment for the Invincible Girls Club. They were ready and willing to fight for our right to play kickball and prove to the boys that girls are able to do whatever job we want.

"I have the perfect plan," I told them after school.

"I love the phrase 'perfect plan,'" Myka said. "What do you have in mind?"

"Yes, do tell!" Ruby said, and eagerly leaned forward as if she already knew it would be good.

"The boys won't let us join in their kickball game, so I was thinking, what if we got there first? We could claim the field and not let *them* play in *our* game."

"That's perfect!" Myka said, and clapped her hands together in excitement. "We stop them before they can stop us!"

"Exactly," I said, and took a bow. My plan was brilliant, if I did say so myself.

We didn't waste any time. Why let the boys control the field any longer than necessary? We decided that we'd put the plan into action the next day.

And the following morning we quietly spread the word through the class. The rest of the girls immediately agreed to help, after they learned what had happened the day before. So then all of us girls were practically jumping out of our seats. The boys noticed, but none of them had any idea what was going on. And that made it a million times better.

"What's up with all of you?" Miss Taylor asked, noticing our energy.

Myka shrugged like it was no big deal. "Getting ready for the big game."

Around me, some of my classmates giggled, happy to be in on the plan.

"I hope your big game gets some of your energy out," Miss Taylor said, and before anyone could ask about the game, the bell for lunch rang. "Walk *slowly* to the cafeteria. Save the running for outside."

"Oh, we will," I said, and wiggled my eyebrows up and down like a villain in one of those old cartoons that my stepdad, Scott, thought were so funny.

Lunch seemed to stretch on forever. But finally Ms. Wamelink, the lunch monitor, began to dismiss each table.

"Remember," I whispered to the girls sitting around me. "When it's our turn to go, we need to race to the field."

The girls grinned and gave me thumbs-up.

"All right, table seven, you can leave," Ms. Wamelink told us.

Before she'd even finished talking, every single girl was on her feet.

And wow, was it a sight to see!

We bolted toward the door before the boys could even comprehend what was happening. We ran like racehorses let out of the gate.

Our group whooped and hollered all the way to the field. I pumped my fist in the air and cheered.

"We are the recess all-stars! Let's show them what we've got!" Myka yelled.

We divided up into teams and wasted no time starting our game.

There were two girls on base when the boys realized what was going on. They ran toward the field the same way we had, but this time no one cheered or pumped their fists.

"What are you doing on our field?" Nelson asked.

I made a big deal of looking around me.

"Hmm . . . funny, I don't see a sign that says this is *your* field." I turned to Ruby. "Do you see anything that says that?"

Ruby shook her head. "Nope, not a thing!"

I faced the boys with my hands on my hips. "We're trying to play a game of kickball. Do you mind stepping aside so you're not blocking our bases?"

We didn't wait for a response. We started to play again, and the boys quickly learned that if they didn't get out of our way, they'd get bonked on the head with a ball or pushed over by one of us racing toward base.

They walked away in a daze. I was positive none of them understood what had just happened.

"Okay, who's up next?" I shouted as if this were what we always did at recess.

And do you know something?

I totally wanted it to be something we always did at recess.

Kickball was fun!

Really fun!

I understood why the boys raced out there every day after lunch.

And I wanted to be a part of it.

We played through recess, and when we came back into class, we could not stop talking about how great it had been.

"It looks like you had a wonderful recess!" Miss Taylor said.

"It wasn't wonderful at all," Brady announced, his face scrunched and angry.

"We had an amazing time," I said, and the rest of the girls in the class nodded.

"A super-stupendous time! We played kick-ball," Myka said.

"You took our field," Brady yelled.

"Like we said, your name wasn't anywhere on that field," Ruby reminded him.

"Okay, okay, that's enough," Miss Taylor said.

"I hope you had fun," Nelson said. "Because it's the last time you'll use the field."

That got everyone worked up, and soon we were arguing over each other.

"Class! Settle down!" Miss Taylor called out.

That was when I got another brilliant idea. The perfect solution to who got to use the field. It was so brilliant that I could hardly sit still for the rest of the day. It was *not* easy to stay settled.

"All right, hear me out," I told Brady as we headed toward the buses. "We're both arguing over who owns the field. A field some of you claim to have dibs on, when you very well know that isn't true. But what if there were a name on it?"

"What do you mean?" Brady asked.

"The girls should play a game against the boys. And the winner of that game earns control over the field. Forever."

"Forever?" Brady asked.

"Forever," I confirmed.

Brady began to laugh.

"Laugh all you want," I told him. "But we'll be the ones laughing the most when we take over the field."

"All right," Brady said, and stuck his hand out. "You've got yourself a deal. I'll fill the other boys in on the plan on Monday."

I took his hand and shook. "And may the best *woman* win."

4 NO PLACE LIKE HOME

Uncle Patrick's cupcake shop, Sprinkle & Shine, was almost always open for business. If you wanted a cupcake, chances were that you could walk in and take your pick of all his delicious flavors. And believe me, my friends and I did it often. Sometimes too often, but how could we resist mini cupcakes? It was pretty much impossible!

However, if you wanted a cupcake on Sunday, forget about it. Because Sunday was family time.

Or what Uncle Patrick called Imad's Sports Extravaganza Night. The shop closed early, then reopened its doors for the truest of true fans of football, baseball, and basketball; sometimes all three at the same time, depending on the time of year!

Because while Uncle Patrick loved cupcakes, Uncle Imad's obsession was sports. He never missed the chance to remind us that he'd played three varsity sports in high school and still held a state record in swimming. He had season tickets for football, and when he traveled with Uncle Patrick, the two of them always tried to see a game at the stadium in that city. They even had pennants hanging in their house from all the stadiums they'd visited.

While Mom and Scott were strict about screen time, they made an exception for Imad's Sports Extravaganza Night. Which was a good thing, because Sprinkle & Shine didn't just have one screen turned on. Nope, usually there were three or four screens—the two screens mounted on the walls, and one or two more that Uncle Imad set up on the counter, depending on what teams were playing. He muted the TVs so no one would get confused from the mix of noise. Besides, we made enough noise just by ourselves. Between the yelling, cheering, and calling plays, you wouldn't have been able to hear the game even if you'd tried.

I grabbed a nacho from the giant pile in the middle of the table. Uncle Imad called them his kitchen-sink nachos. We each brought leftovers from home, and then he would put a bag of chips on a cookie sheet and dump "everything but the kitchen sink" on top. If it was a leftover in either of our fridges, it almost always made its way onto the nachos.

"This is amazing," I said after I took a bite. I eyed the pile of chips and tried to figure out what was on it. I saw the previous night's mac and cheese, some chili, hash browns, and pieces of bacon. Then, on top of it all was tons and tons of melted cheese. Uncle Imad believed that everything tasted amazing with cheese on it, and anyone who ate his kitchen-sink nachos had to agree.

Tonight we had on two baseball games and a football game.

"There's the pitch. It's a little bit outside, and . . . ball!" I yelled.

The umpire's left hand indicated a ball, and when the display on the bottom of the TV confirmed it, I grinned at my family.

"Second pitch is a low fastball right toward the bat. Strike one!" I said before the umpire signaled what the next pitch was.

"Ball!" Carter said at the same time, and I rolled my eyes.

"There's no way that wasn't a strike," I said.

"Are you kidding me? It was too low on the right!" he argued, but stopped when the umpire raised his right hand for a strike.

I shot Carter a look of victory and turned back

to the game. I called the next two pitches, each of them correctly.

"And that's the inning!" I said as the batter walked back to the dugout. I rubbed both hands together. "What can I say? I'm the ultimate pro at calling games."

"I gotta hand it to you, you're good," Scott said.

"That's why I'm going to be the world's best sports announcer," I said.

"I wouldn't go that far," Carter said.

"Is that a challenge?" I asked. "Because I accept. Watch me work my magic!"

I continued to call the plays, talk about players' stats in between, and share knowledge that I had about the teams.

"Are you convinced yet?" I asked Carter when a commercial came on.

"I am! That was fantastic!" Uncle Imad said, and my family nodded in agreement.

"I'd say that you made it pretty obvious that you do have what it takes, Lulu," Scott said.

"Watch out, Charley Mosk. Lauren is here and ready to take over your job!" I said, but I was totally joking. No one could ever be as good as Mosk. He was on the radio every morning, talking sports, sports, sports. He was also the voice of Friday Night Lights for our high school, where he'd graduated about twenty years before. He broadcast the livestreams of our high school's games.

"That's it!" I shouted. "I'll do the football broadcast!"

Like a lightning bolt, another brilliant idea had come to me. I was on a winning streak of great ideas!

"You're good, Lauren, but I doubt Mosk is stepping aside anytime soon," Uncle Imad said as he grabbed a nacho and scooped up some more of the toppings that were on the cookie sheet.

"No, I'm not going to take his job. I'm going to shadow him for our career unit!" I said.

"Huh?" Carter asked, shoving more nachos into his mouth.

"Are you looking for a job?" Scott asked. "Because if you are, I'd like to hire a dishwasher, duster, and toilet scrubber."

Mom playfully threw a balled-up napkin at Scott. "Those are your chores, and you can't outsource them to someone else."

"It doesn't hurt to try!" Scott said as he held up his hands in surrender.

"I'm not looking for a job," I said to get the conversation back on track. "We're supposed to shadow someone for our career unit and then give a presentation about our experience. Maybe Mosk would let me sit in the press booth at the football game this Friday."

"You don't want to shadow a vet?" Mom asked. "Or someone at the dog shelter?"

"I would, but I get to spend time with the dogs every Saturday, and I already know I love that. I'm more interested in trying something new that I might be good at," I told her. "Besides, I have something to prove to a bunch of boys who don't think girls can play kickball or broadcast sports."

"Ooooh, I like a good plan to prove the doubters wrong! You know I always have your back!" Uncle Patrick told me.

"Yep, I know you always do!" I said, and the two of us high-fived. I turned to Mom and Scott. "Can I do it?"

"I don't see why not," Mom said. "As long as Mosk is okay with it."

"Could we email him?" I asked.

"Sure, I'll track down his email tomorrow," Mom said, but I shook my head.

"Could you do it now, please? This is going to be epic!" I said.

"Wow, you don't waste any time. My little go-getter," Mom said proudly.

"You can use my work computer to ask him," Uncle Patrick said, and the three of us headed toward his back office and took a seat around his desk. He got the computer up and going, and

Mom found Mosk's email on the radio website and typed it into a new message.

"Okay, you're set," she said. "Make sure he knows you're writing from my account and how old you are and where you go to school."

"Will do," I said. I typed out the email and made sure to make it sound professional and polite. I really wanted Mosk to let me shadow

him, so I tried my best to sound like someone who was mature. I asked Mom and Uncle Patrick to read it over when I was done.

After they made a few fixes, Mom said, "This looks great. I can't imagine him not agreeing to your request."

"I sure hope he does," I said, and clicked send, ready to show Mosk and the world what I could do.

FOUL BALL

We made an agreement with the boys. We would switch who got the field every other day to practice before the big game. The girls got the field first.

"It's not like we need to practice. We've got this," Nelson bragged during class, but I simply rolled my eyes. We'd see about that.

As we girls made our way to the field after lunch on Monday, I had a plan for how we would use our time.

The pressure was on.

If we didn't win, we'd never step onto the field again.

We needed to take this seriously, but after playing for a few minutes, I wasn't sure the rest of the girls felt the same way.

"You need to call for it!" I shouted when two girls bumped into each other in the outfield and landed in the grass, laughing.

"Throw the ball to second!" I shouted to Emelyn as Tyra headed toward second base. Emelyn tilted her head as if she couldn't hear me. Tyra stepped onto second base and continued to third. "Ugh! You could have easily gotten her out."

"Don't kick the ball straight into the air!" I yelled to Rhiannon, who made the ball go up and then easily down into someone's hands every time she practiced kicking.

It went on like that again and again; one of my classmates would kick the ball straight up into the air, and someone would chase after it and then let it fall to the ground in an awful attempt to catch it. Or someone would be able to get a runner out easily but instead would hold on to the ball and not throw it.

"Tag her out!" I screamed, but it fell on deaf ears. Myka was the only one who seemed to be trying.

Everyone else seemed to have checked out from the game. Two of my classmates even sat in the grass braiding each other's hair. It was as if they didn't even care.

"Pay attention!" I shouted, and it may have been a little too loud, but I was mad. "Do you like this field? Because if we don't start practicing, the boys are going to be the only ones using it. Ever!"

So maybe that last part had been a bit dramatic, but I didn't know how else to get them to listen.

Before I could say anything more, the bell rang, signaling the end of recess.

I threw my hands up in the air in frustration.

"Great! We wasted an entire practice!" I said to my friends as we headed back toward the school. "Not that it mattered. Myka was the only one who listened."

"It was hard to listen," Emelyn said in a soft voice.

"Hard to listen? I was giving instructions the entire time," I said.

"Yelling them was more like it," Ruby said.

"She's right," Myka agreed. "I wouldn't want to be on a team if all my coaches did was yell."

"I'm trying to get us the field," I argued.

"It was a bit intense," Ruby said.

"Remember, if we don't win, we're never going to be able to play on the field again," I told my friends.

"But does that matter, if no one wants to be on it?" Ruby asked. "I'm not trying to be mean, but today wasn't fun."

"Sometimes you have to work hard at what you want," I protested.

"It's not always about winning," Myka said. "For me, playing is the part that I love."

"But we won't get to play if we don't win," I said, and glanced back at the field as we walked away, worried that if I couldn't convince the girls to get serious, that might be one of our last times playing on it.

ONE HABIT I'LL NEVER KICK

Mom and Scott made it a rule that we tried to eat dinner together every night.

"Family time is the most important time!" Scott would say. "And everyone has to eat, so why not do it together?"

Scott was an amazing cook, and we had some of our best conversations at the dinner table. However, once Carter joined the cross-country team, it got harder to sit down together. Mom didn't get home until six-fifteen and Carter had practice at seven p.m. three times a week. So, Scott came up with a great solution. Every Tuesday and Thursday, we had family dinner in our minivan!

I'm not kidding.

"If you can't bring everyone to the table," Scott would say, "we'll bring the table to you."

And that's exactly what he did during the tiny window of time we were all home before Carter's practice. Scott made the most of it. No one was allowed to schedule anything during those forty-five minutes.

He cooked dinner and packed it into containers for us, complete with napkins, silverware, a drink, and cookies. An official home-cooked dinner with the six food groups, as Scott always said. "Bread, meat, fruits and veggies, dairy, fat, and cookies!"

"Cookies are not a food group," Mom would say, but we always overruled her. When it was three against one, cookies most definitely were a food group in our house and were included in every family dinner.

Then, in between picking up Mom from work and dropping Carter off at cross-country, we somehow managed to have a family dinner. It wasn't fancy. It could get a bit messy. But I wouldn't change it for anything, because like Scott said, "Family time is the most important time!"

And eating in the minivan allowed us to be together.

"Ow, Carter! Be careful," I said as he climbed into the van. "Your elbow hit me in the shoulder."

That was how things went in my family. Mom called us her beautiful chaos.

Scott drove to the middle school parking lot and pulled into a spot near the stadium. Mom passed out the packed containers of our dinner, and we settled in for our unique and creative version of family dinner night.

"What's the best thing that happened to you

today?" Scott asked as he took a bite of one of his meatballs. It was the question he always started with after making sure the car radio was off and screens were put away, so we could spend those forty minutes connecting as a family.

"It was calzone day in the cafeteria," I said. "You can't get better than that."

"I found a five-dollar bill in the parking lot," Carter said, and did a happy shimmy in his seat.

"I rocked our spelling test," I added.

"We played an intense game of four on four during gym," Carter said as he shoveled spaghetti into his mouth. "We had the other team begging for mercy by the end."

"Who won?" I asked.

He shrugged. "No idea. We didn't keep score. We never do."

"Why not?" I asked, surprised.

"I don't know. People don't always play to win," Carter said.

"But everything is a competition in our house," I argued. It was true. When I said "everything," I meant *everything*. Just the other day, Carter and I had tried to see which one of us could do the most burps in a row. Mom had put a stop to that fast, but I'm sure I would've won.

"That's because we're siblings," Carter reasoned. "It's like a law that we have to compete. I mean, how else would we declare the king of doing the most push-ups or taking the fastest shower?"

"Um, you mean 'the queen of push-ups,'" I corrected him. "And we know you take the fastest shower. Or should I say, we can *smell* that you take the fastest shower."

"Competitions are exciting, but everything doesn't need to be one," Mom said. "There's nothing wrong with playing a game for fun."

"But what if you need to win?" I said as I thought about the kickball field.

Scott shrugged and then spoke up. "Then walk away. It's not worth battling over. You never *need* to win anything."

But he was wrong. If we walked away from the kickball game, the girls would walk away from the field forever.

"Whoa, whoa, whoa," Carter said, and grabbed the container away that I was reaching for. "You've already had a bunch of garlic bread. I want that last piece."

"And so do I," I said, my mouth watering as I thought about the buttery deliciousness.

"Should we rock, paper, scissors for it?" Carter asked.

"Wait a minute. I thought you said games weren't fun when there were winners or losers," I teased.

"Oh, this isn't a game. This is garlic bread," Carter said in a very serious tone.

I reached out and grabbed the bread. "Well, according to Scott, sometimes it's not worth battling over."

I took a big bite and grinned.

"You got me there," Carter said. "That piece is all yours."

I chewed the bread slowly. I didn't care what Carter and Scott had said about not playing to win. The taste of victory was delicious.

THERE'S NO *I* IN TEAM

When it was our turn on the field again, the girls didn't exactly race there like they had the last time. In fact, it was the opposite. You would have thought they were on their way to take a spelling test or complete a million math problems. It was obvious no one but Myka and me wanted to be there.

I guess the bright side was that they were there, even if they weren't happy about it.

But I had a plan to pull the team back together.

I thought about what my friends had said after our first practice, and about the conversation with my family.

After our disastrous practice, the girls needed to get excited to simply have fun again.

When Carter and I fought, Mom and Scott did one of the worst things you could do. They turned off the Wi-Fi. The only way we could get it back was to work together. And working together meant doing team-building activities. Super-silly ones that Scott had used when he was a camp counselor. He'd make us all—yep, him and Mom, too—do games where we had to line up according to birthday month without talking, or grasp each other's hands and form a human pretzel that we then had to untangle without letting go. By the end of Scott's activities, we'd be on the ground in a fit of laughter, and usually no one would remember what we had even fought about.

If Scott could get fighting siblings to work together and turn a bad situation into something fun, I hoped I'd be able to do the same with the girls on the kickball field.

"We are going to do something a little different," I said as my voice cracked from nerves. I really wanted to pull this off, but I was scared that I had turned the girls against wanting to play kickball ever again. I tried to tell myself that the fact that they had shown up was a good thing, and that gave me the push to keep talking. "I mean, if that's okay with you. I don't think our last practice went that well."

A bunch of the girls nodded in agreement, which didn't make things easier.

"I owe you an apology," I told the group. It was scary to admit I'd been wrong, in front of a ton of people. "I'm sorry. I got a bit carried away. I hate when people tell me I can't do something, so all I was thinking about was winning possession of the field."

"We do want that," Rhiannon said. "But we also want to have fun."

"I get that now," I said. "I really do. That's why we're going to do things a little differently to prepare for the game."

I nodded at Emelyn, Myka, and Ruby, and the three of them opened the tote bags they had helped me carry to the field. We had talked about my plan the day before, and they were confident it would work.

"Okay, first we need fuel." I reached into one of the bags and pulled out oatmeal cream pies wrapped in plastic. "I brought enough that you can have a few, because, really, part of having fun is eating as many sweet things as you want. And for those of you who are a little healthier, there are oranges in the other bag, along with juice boxes and bottled water. Help yourselves!"

"You don't have to tell me twice!" Tyra said, and grabbed some of the treats. The rest of the girls rushed over too, because it was impossible to resist an oatmeal cream pie!

"Now that we have fuel," I said as everyone

dug into their treats, "it's time to celebrate! My favorite sports announcer, Charley Mosk, says the best teams are the ones that celebrate each other on and off the field. So let's share! Big or small, what's something awesome that happened lately?"

Myka shot her hand into the air. "Oh, oh! I'll go first! This morning I got the last cinnamon-raisin bagel. Everyone else had to eat plain ones."

Ruby wrinkled her nose. "Yep, cinnamon is a much better choice."

"You're right about that," I said, and turned to Emelyn next to me. "What can you celebrate?"

Emelyn chewed on her bottom lip for a moment. Then she grabbed two sections of her hair and pulled them away from her ears to show off some beaded earrings. "I'm celebrating my newest creation. I made them yesterday and love how they turned out."

She was right. Her earrings were supercool, and we might not have noticed them if we hadn't done this activity. One by one my class-mates shared things about themselves. Some of the celebrations were big, like for Tyra, who had gotten 100 percent on the science quiz, and some were small and quiet, like for Rhiannon, who shared that she'd surprised her mom the night before by making dinner. We talked and ate our snacks and laughed. The group was together again, and it felt good.

"Okay, time to head onto the field," I said, and everyone got up, but a few of the girls exchanged looks. "Don't worry. This won't be painful. In fact, we're not even going to play kickball."

"Not play kickball?" Kara asked. "I thought the whole idea to having the field was to practice."

"Nope, but we are going to connect as a team. So what I need you to do is split into two groups." Everyone followed my directions, and I gave each group two jump ropes that I had tied together. "Okay, spread your jump ropes out on the ground so that they make a circle."

Tyra looked at me, confused. "Um, what does this have to do with kickball?"

"Trust me. You're going to have to give this a shot, and I promise it will be worth it." I took in their confused faces and hoped that what I was saying was true. I mean, it worked with my brother and me, so hopefully the same would happen here. "What you need to do with your group is get everyone inside the jump-rope circle. No one can be outside it."

My classmates looked at me with raised eyebrows and confusion for a moment, but then Ruby shrugged and stepped inside her team's circle.

"Easy!" she said, and beckoned to the other girls to join her. "Get in here, everyone."

Once they were in the circles, I nodded and told both groups to step back out. I went over to the circles and made them smaller, taking away about a fourth of the space.

"Okay, fit your group into the new circle," I instructed, and once again the girls stepped inside. It was a bit of a tight fit, but still possible without much effort.

"I bet I know what's going to happen next," Tyra said.

I took away one of the jump ropes from each group, so now the circles were small.

"You've got this," I told everyone.

It took a bit of laughter, but soon both groups smooshed super close together so that they could fit in the circle.

"We did it!" Myka cheered when her group was in.

"For a second," Ruby agreed as they tumbled to the grass in a pile.

"Are you ready for the last task?" I asked, and rubbed my hands together. This was always the best part. I couldn't wait to see how the girls tried to make this happen.

I picked up one of the jump ropes and pointed at the remaining one. "All right, I need all of you to get in there!"

"All of us?" Corrine asked, her eyes wide.

"We can stop, if you're not up to the challenge—" I started.

"Oh, we've got this," Myka interrupted. "Let's show her!"

The girls tried over and over again and continued to fall into giggling heaps on the ground, their arms and legs tangled up together.

"This is impossible," Tyra called to me as they scrambled to figure out how to fit everyone into their circle.

Finally Rhiannon suggested they do piggybacks, and soon half of them had climbed onto the backs of the other girls. They were smooshed together, but everyone was in the circle. I half expected Ms. Kratus to come running at us, blowing her whistle and yelling about safety, but she was too busy keeping the boys off the swings.

At least Myka and I weren't the only ones who couldn't go high.

"We did it!" Ruby cheered before they tumbled down.

"Timber!" Tyra called, which started everyone laughing again.

"Way to think outside the box!" I said.

"Or outside the circle," Ruby corrected me, which got a bunch of groans.

As the girls excitedly discussed what they had just done, I sat back and watched. This was the attitude we needed. This was the fun that was supposed to be a part of playing kickball. The feeling we'd lost when I'd made it too competitive. I had forgotten that it was only a game and that sometimes there were enough oatmeal cream pies for everyone.

A GAME CHANGER

While our dinners were full of conversation and laugher, breakfast at my house was super low-key.

That was because we had a secret weapon that kept everyone quiet.

A secret weapon called Charley Mosk.

We listened to him every morning, and it was an unspoken rule that we gave him our attention.

"Morning, Lulu!" Scott said as I sat at the kitchen table. The smell of coffee and bacon hung

in the air, and my stomach rumbled. I grabbed a

piece of bacon and popped it into my mouth.

"Playing kickball really takes a lot out of you," I said.

"Try running cross-country," Carter said as he walked into the kitchen. He held up his fitness tracker and waved his wrist around. "Yesterday I had almost thirty thousand steps. Pretty sure that's a record or something."

Instead of responding, I picked up a banana and held it to my ear like a phone. "Hello, hello, is this the Guinness World Records? I'd like to report my stepbrother for the most steps ever walked by someone."

"Ha ha," Carter said. "You want to wear this today and track your steps? Let's see who walks the most."

"I wouldn't want to embarrass you," I said.

Scott turned up the radio to drown out our teasing, and Charley Mosk's voice filled the kitchen. We had him on so often, it was as if he were our fifth family member.

"Now, this is how to start the morning," Scott said as he settled into his chair and took a big sip of coffee. "Charley talking sports and a steaming cup of hot coffee."

"Yeah, I think you forgot something in your coffee," Mom said as she entered the room and poured her own mug. She dumped what appeared to be about ten spoonfuls of sugar into the coffee and lightened it with cream. Why they drank that gross stuff was beyond me, but Mom always said coffee was what made the world go round.

"There's no reason to mess with perfect," Scott said, and took a long sip out of his mug.

As the two of them argued about the best way to drink coffee, I tried to listen to the radio. The problem was, I could only make out every few words because of the racket Scott and Mom were making. That's why, when Charley said my name, I thought I was hearing things.

"Um, everyone," I said. "You're not going to believe this, but I swear Charley mentioned me."

Carter laughed so hard, he spit orange juice out of his mouth.

"I'm not joking," I insisted. "Stay quiet for a second."

Scott turned the volume up, and we listened as Charley talked about the high school games this week and his pick for the winners.

"We'll have to wait and see what happens when we meet under the lights," Charley said, and chuckled. "So, Lauren, if you're listening, I'd love to have you shadow me. Who knows, maybe you can take over my job! It's about time I thought about retiring. A deserted island, lounging in a hammock, surrounded by crystal-blue water sounds perfect."

I turned to my family with wide eyes.

"You heard that, right?" I asked. "I'm not hearing things, am I?"

"If you are, then I am too," Scott said. "Congratulations, Lulu! You got yourself an invite to one of the best seats in the house at the Erie High School stadium."

"This is incredible! Mosk said yes!" I squealed, and shook my head in disbelief.

"Oh, honey, you're going to do such a great job," Mom said. "And Charley has had people in his studio before to help him broadcast games and talk sports. I have a feeling we might be hearing your voice on air."

"I'm shadowing him, not broadcasting," I stressed to them. "There's a big difference between watching someone else talk on air and talking yourself."

I tried to be firm, but as they shared a look with each other, I gulped. Could they be right? Would Charley have me talk on the air? And if he did, was I ready for that?

9 PRACTICE MAKES PERFECT

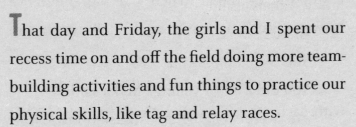

That day and Friday, the girls and I spent our recess time on and off the field doing more team-building activities and fun things to practice our physical skills, like tag and relay races.

Yep, you heard that right.

We didn't play kickball. Instead Scott continued to teach me new games, and I had the girls focus on different athletic activities that Myka led using what she'd learned in soccer. We grew as a team *and* improved our kickball skills, but without the pressure that had been there before. And our time together was filled with laughter, smiles, and working together.

While we weren't technically preparing for the game, I was positive we had what it took to work as a team and win control of the field.

"I gotta hand it to you, Lauren," Ruby said after recess Friday. "I didn't think this was going to work, after that first practice."

"Yeah, not to be mean, but I was ready to walk away," Emelyn said.

I stared at her in surprise.

"You were not," I said.

"You did a lot of yelling," Myka said.

"We were heading for disaster fast," Ruby said, but then quickly added, "It's not like that anymore. Now I can't wait for recess!"

Maybe fun was exactly what the team needed. Maybe Carter was right and you didn't always need to play to win. Or in our case, play at all. Maybe sometimes you simply needed to have fun and be silly, because when you did, the team part came together by itself.

"I'm glad you stuck it out," I said. "And I'm glad you told me how awful I was being, so I could change things."

"Let's just say Myka, Emelyn, and I are the reason the girls are going to win the field," Ruby joked as we took our seats in our classroom.

"You can have the credit," I said. "I'll take the win any way that I can!"

"Nah, it's all you," Emelyn said. "You pulled our team back together, and we are going to serve up a win!"

"Um, I think she means kick up a win," Myka corrected her.

"As long as you don't kick it straight into the other team's hands, you're good!" I added to their jokes. Soon the four of us were laughing so hard that Miss Taylor came over and tapped on our desks to remind us to focus.

"Recess is over, girls. Let's get back to work," she said.

We turned to our papers and did exactly that.

Well, until Nelson threw something across the aisle that hit me in the arm.

"Ouch!" I said, and narrowed my eyes at him. "What did you do that for?"

He leaned toward me so he could whisper, "We should have gotten the practice field today."

"Today was our day," I reminded him. "We agreed on every other day. Why would you have gotten it?"

"Because you never use it," he said.

"What's that supposed to mean?" I asked.

"None of you were even playing today. Why should you get the field if you aren't going to practice on it?"

"Who said we weren't practicing?"

"Eating snacks and jumping around is not practicing. You do the exact same thing on the blacktop when it's not your turn on the field," Nelson said. "It doesn't seem right that you're allowed to take up time on the field if you're not even using it for the right reasons."

"We know exactly what we're doing," I told him.

"Yeah, a whole lot of nothing," he said, as his face grew more and more red. He was losing his temper.

"If you say so," I said, and shrugged as if it were no big deal, which made it an even bigger deal to him. "Maybe we're preparing our secret weapon."

Nelson ran his hands through his hair in frustration. "What's that supposed to mean?"

"Focus on your own team," I said. "I've got mine under control. All will be revealed on game day when we unleash our secret weapon. Now, I'm trying to get this worksheet done, so if you could let me get back to that, I'd appreciate it."

The funny thing was that we really did have a secret weapon. It might have looked like we weren't practicing, but when you had a team that worked together, you were unstoppable. And I couldn't wait to see the boys try to change that.

PREGAME JITTERS

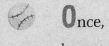

Once, when I was younger, I thought it would be a good idea to bring a jar full of fireflies into the house without telling anyone. I left it in my room and forgot about it when I got up to use the bathroom. I kicked the jar over, and the cap fell off. My room was full of what seemed like a million flickering lights.

I thought of that moment as I stood in the broadcaster's box that evening at the high school football game.

I was at the same height as the giant lights that spilled down over the field. In the stands, the screens of people's phones lit on and off like the bright bursts of nerves that flickered in my stomach.

Myka bumped her hip into mine. "Are you ready for this?"

"Nope," I said, because being up there made it real.

"You're going to be the true MVP of the game," Myka said, and I groaned at her awful joke.

"We'll send good vibes to you from the bleachers," Emelyn said, and took my hand and squeezed it. I squeezed back.

"All right, girls," Scott said as he held his phone up to show us the time. "The game is starting soon. Our Lauren fan club needs to head to their seats."

"But we'll be with you the whole time," Mom said. "Listening, that is!"

Emelyn dug into her tote bag and pulled out

a phone. "Yep! My mom said I could listen to the broadcast of the game on her phone."

"And I borrowed Jordan's earbuds, so the two of us will each use one to listen," Myka said.

"And Ruby can use my phone, because I plan to snuggle up to your mom and share a set of earbuds too," Scott said, and wrapped his arm around Mom and pulled her close.

Mom wiggled out from under his arm and turned to Charley Mosk. "Thanks again for giving my daughter this opportunity."

"No, thank *you*," he replied. "Lauren and I are going to make some broadcasting magic tonight."

"Prepare to be amazed," said Myka, my biggest fan. "Whenever Lauren comes with me to watch my brothers' games, she calls the plays. She knows what she's talking about."

I loved that everyone believed in me, but I was still nervous.

Mom gave me one last hug and whispered

into my ear, "You've got this. Don't you worry about a thing."

The group left with wishes of luck. I held on to Mom's words and believed them with all my might. Myka was right. I *did* know what I was doing. I *would* be fine.

"Okay, first things first," Charley said, and pointed to a black swivel chair right at the middle of the desk in front of the giant glass window. "I need you to sit in that chair."

"Isn't that your seat?" I asked. I had expected to sit off to the side, maybe in a corner, and watch things from afar. I'd never expected to be in the middle of the action, let alone where he usually sat.

"Nope, tonight it's got your name on it. I want you front and center in the captai⌐ ⌐ seat. Go ahead, sit down!"

So I did, and he adjus⌐ ⌐e height to make sure I could see out ⌐ ⌐dow.

"We have the best view in the house," I said.

"You'd better believe it. Why do you think I come back every week to announce the game? It's my little secret that I refuse to share with the other Timber Wolves fans. If I did, this room would be packed!" Charley said, and chuckled. He held up a pair of headphones.

"Put these on. They block the noise around us so we can focus on the game and hear each other."

"You mean so I can hear what *you're* saying, right?" I asked.

"No way. When you're in the broadcaster's box, you're broadcasting. That's the rule."

"I'm only supposed to shadow you, which means I watch and stay out of the way."

"No can do. I need a copilot. It gets lonely hearing myself talk."

I swallowed. "I'm not sure I can talk to this entire crowd."

"I'm confident that you can do it here. Trust you can do it at home, I wouldn't put you on the air if I didn't think you could handle this."

"If you say so," I said, but I had my doubts. I had thought I was going to sit there and watch him do his job. Wasn't that what shadowing was supposed to be? My classmates who were shadowing doctors weren't doing surgery, and those shadowing hairstylists weren't cutting hair.

"All right, we're ready to go," he said. "I'm about to switch the microphone on, so make sure you don't say anything you don't want everyone to hear."

"Everyone?" I asked, my eyes wide.

"Well, anyone who tunes into the livestream. It's usually a few hundred people."

I think he said that to make me feel better. But even though that number might not have been big compared to who listened to his morning radio show, to me, a few hundred listeners felt like a million. There was nothing about that number that calmed my nerves. Nothing at all.

"Speak when you feel comfortable, and listen

when you don't. Once we go live, we're live until a time-out and I play a commercial. That's one of the hardest parts. You need to fill the time. If you stop talking, there's nothing. Follow my lead. I'll give you plenty of stuff to talk about."

"Okay," I said, the pressure to do well growing more intense with each thing he said.

"Great. We're live in three, two, one!" He clicked a button on the computer, and a red light came on; we could be heard from anywhere. That was both terrifying and cool at the same time.

"Hello, Timber Wolves country. This is Charley Mosk coming at you live from under the Friday Night Lights. Erie High School is about to take on the Chesterfield Stallions. Tonight I have a surprise. I'd like to introduce a special guest. I have Lauren Connors broadcasting with me. You may or may not know her as one of the founding members of the Invincible Girls Club, a group of third graders making some incredible changes in our community. Lauren helped find older shelter dogs forever homes, but that's not her only talent. She also knows a lot about sports. I'm looking forward to hearing her opinions tonight, as I'm sure you are too." Then Charley turned his chair toward me, and I broke out in a sweat. "What do you think, Lauren? How is this game going to go?"

My voice was stuck in my throat. I couldn't speak. All I could focus on was the dead air and the little voice inside me telling me to speak up, speak up, speak up. But it was impossible. Because there was another voice that reminded me of how my classmates had laughed when I'd announced what I wanted to do. Maybe they had been right, because at the moment I was doing an awful job of broadcasting anything.

Then I thought of my family and how no one had found it was odd when I'd told them I wanted to shadow Charley. They'd agreed that it was a good idea. They'd encouraged me. I thought about how my friends were in the stands right now to support me and how Uncle Patrick and

Uncle Imad had friends at Sprinkle & Shine listening to the broadcast.

That was enough to break me out of my spell.

"We have a very good chance," I told him. The words came out fast and shaky. I thought about the conversations Myka and I had had about the two teams. How she'd filled me in on her brothers' thoughts too. I took a breath and spoke louder, slower. "But we need to make sure our defense is focused. Chesterfield has some of the best offense in the conference, and if we aren't ready for that, we aren't making anything good happen. The Wolves need to be about three steps ahead of them and anticipate their plays so we can stop them. If we can do that, which I believe we can, I have no doubt we'll come out on top."

Charley gave me a thumbs-up and grinned. "I couldn't have said it better," he said. "In fact, you might have said it better."

I wasn't so sure about that, but his encouragement felt good.

"Okay, folks, the team is taking the field. You couldn't have asked for a better night. Not a cloud in the sky, and there's a slight breeze. We need to remember this weather come late October when everyone is freezing in the stands."

"Speak for yourself," I joked. "You get to be up in the warm box. The rest of us will be shivering down below, watching as the team moves toward the playoffs."

Charley and I went back and forth the entire

first two quarters. It became easier and easier as the game went on. "You sure you're not trying to take my job from me?" he joked.

"I mean, if I'm the right fit, I guess I would have to say yes," I joked right back.

"I knew it! Your plan was to take over," he said.

"Yep, so you'd better watch out!" It was fun up there, and I most certainly didn't want it to be my last night in the box.

We went to commercial, and Charley turned to me. "It's time," he said.

"Time for what?"

"Time for me to turn off my microphone and let you call some of the game yourself!"

I looked at him as if he had lost his mind. "There's no way I can call the game myself," I protested.

"Oh, but you can," he said. "You've done a great job so far, and part of being a sports broadcaster is carrying the game on your own. You don't always get a co-host when you're on the air.

"I promise you can handle it," he continued. "Let the commercial finish running once the time-out ends, and then press the button on the right of the screen to get us broadcasting again." He scooted his chair all the way into the back corner.

And just like that, I was left alone in the broadcaster's seat, about to go on the air.

Solo.

KNOCKING IT OUT OF THE PARK

The reality of what had just happened sank in.

What was I going to do?

How could I broadcast alone?

I glanced over at Charley, and he gave me a thumbs-up.

I eyed the door and for a quick moment considered running out and never looking back. But that would only have created bigger problems, and the Invincible Girls were not quitters.

On the field the teams broke from their

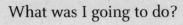

huddles and went back to their positions. The time-out was over, which meant I would need to press that red button and talk or there was going to be nothing but dead air.

I dragged the cursor toward the button as if it were a giant spider that I most certainly didn't want to touch. I closed my eyes, gave myself an internal pep talk, and quickly clicked the mouse button.

A red light came on.

I was back on the air.

Terrified.

I might have only been eight, but I'd done some wild things in my life so far. My family had gone white water rafting, I'd zip-lined over trees, and I'd even swum in the ocean with a ton of stingrays, but none of that compared to this.

I took a shaky breath and spoke into the microphone. "Okay, Timber Wolves fans, we are back, and I have a feeling that this game is about to get a lot more intense. The Wolves are behind, but a touchdown can put us back on top. And I have nothing but faith that that's what we're going to see out there."

I pictured watching games in my family room. I thought about how good I was at calling the plays and how sometimes I'd turn down the volume on the TV and call the game instead of the actual broadcasters. I thought about all of that, and a funny thing happened.

As I continued to tell myself I could do this, that little voice in my head that said I couldn't began to evaporate, until suddenly it wasn't there anymore. It was only me and the microphone and the game, and I wasn't nervous.

I'd thought it would be hard to carry the game myself, but I had learned enough from announcing the game with my family and hanging with Myka that I could fill the spaces when not much was happening on the field. And during those moments when there was a lot going on, the excitement made me forget everything else but what was happening below.

I talked through a bunch of plays, and it wasn't until the other team called a time-out and I switched to a commercial that I realized how long I'd been on the air. The third quarter was almost over, and Charley still hadn't joined me.

"Well done, Lauren. I couldn't have called that better myself," he said, and clapped his hands slowly.

"I can't believe you let me call the game solo for so long," I told him.

"You were in the groove. And when someone is in the groove, you don't distract them."

"I tried my best," I told him.

"You're a natural. You've got talent, Lauren," he said, and my eyes lit up. I imagined myself calling professional games in the future!

"Thanks," I said. "Tonight it was high school football. Next, the Super Bowl! Or maybe the

Puppy Bowl, because then I can mix two of my loves together."

"I wouldn't doubt it," he said, and chuckled as he picked up his headphones and pushed the livestream button. "And we are back after that short commercial break. I don't know if any of you out there noticed, but Lauren carried almost that entire quarter by herself. And she did it like a pro."

We talked, and it looked as if the Timber Wolves were going to win, until the final play, when Chesterfield faked us out and scored.

"Oh my goodness!" Charley yelled, and jumped up. He pointed to the field, his face full of shock. "Did you see that play? It was incredible! Wow!"

"That was pretty amazing," I responded, since we were still on the air, but I was confused about his praise for the other team. That play had lost us the game.

The two of us continued to talk back and forth for a few more minutes to wrap everything up, and then we signed off.

"How was your first sports radio experience?" he asked.

"Incredible," I said. "Thank you so much."

"Careful now. Once you get the broadcasting itch, it's hard to be away from the booth."

"I'm not sure I ever want to be away from this booth too," I said.

"That's what I'm talking about!" he said, grinning.

"There's one thing I'm confused about," I said. "Why did you cheer for Chesterfield? You went nuts when they scored. The game-*winning* score. Aren't you a Timber Wolves fan?"

"Of course I am," Charley said. "But did you see that play? It was incredible. A play like that is worthy of celebrating no matter which team it was."

"I guess," I said, but I wasn't convinced. We'd lost the game. Because of the play Charley had gone wild about. I couldn't imagine being excited about that.

"I'm going to pass on some advice I was given

when I first began to broadcast sports. Now, I wasn't as young as you," he said, and laughed, "but it had a huge influence on the person I am today."

He leaned in toward me.

"The secret is to celebrate the victories of both teams," he said.

"Huh?" That didn't seem right.

"You acknowledge what the other team does well. That's how you can be a great broadcaster that fans from *both* teams want to listen to. If you only cheer for one side, you lose a big part of your audience. So I make sure to talk about all the players and what they do well. I make it feel as if we're a bunch of friends watching football and having a good time."

"You're not upset when the Timber Wolves don't win?" I asked.

"Sure, I'd love for them to win, but I also like any game that's played well, so I give credit where it's due. It makes a loss not as bad, because you can understand why the other team won."

His reasoning sounded kind of like what Carter had said to me in the van the other night. Maybe they were both right. Maybe it really wasn't about who won. Maybe I had it wrong.

"I'll try to do what you do," I said.

"Give it a shot. I think you'll find it's a good way to look at things."

"I will," I promised him.

"I'm going to remind you of that the next time you join me."

"Next time?"

"For sure. I'm expecting you back soon. In fact, what about the next home game? Would love to have you. It gets lonely up here, and you know what you're talking about. I like the sound of 'The Mosk and Lauren Show.'"

"Hmm. . . . 'The Lauren and Mosk Show' sounds better," I joked.

"You've got yourself a deal. Anytime you want to join me, I'm happy to have you be part of *The Lauren and Mosk Show*."

12 A GRAND SLAM IDEA

The final part of our career unit was a presentation about our shadowing experience. We had to present our information in a creative way, and wouldn't you know it, I had another of my brilliant ideas.

"Um, why are you lugging around a giant piece of cardboard?" Myka asked when I got to school. Scott had dropped me off so that I wouldn't have to take the bus. There was no way to easily get the cardboard through the bus doors, up the steps, and into a seat.

"Just you wait. You'll find out soon," I said in a mysterious voice. I was so excited about this that I didn't want to spoil the surprise with anyone.

My friends weren't the only ones wondering about my big piece of cardboard. Miss Taylor had to tell everyone to focus on their work. But it wasn't their fault. I'd feel the same way if I didn't know why there was something large and mysterious sitting in the corner of the classroom.

We reviewed the week's spelling words and did a math lesson, and then it was time to present. Miss Taylor had a cup with our names on Popsicle sticks. She used it to pull out our names one by one instead of calling on us. Usually I didn't want her to pull my name right away, but today I couldn't wait to present.

I wasn't first, though. Or second. Or third. It

wasn't until about half the class had gone that it was my turn.

"Awww, the mystery is about to be revealed. Lauren, you're up," Miss Taylor said.

I jumped from my seat and got my project. I dragged it to the front of the room, careful not to let anyone see the front. The class whispered as I put on a headset and placed the cardboard in front of me.

I then turned to reveal a giant square that Scott had helped me cut into it. It was like I was looking out a window. Or the class was looking at a television screen.

"Hello. I'm Lauren Connors, and I'm coming at you from the Erie High School stadium, where our own Timber Wolves are ready to take on the Chesterfield Stallions. The Timber Wolves have been practicing nonstop this week, and we're hoping that they'll have those Stallions racing back to their school."

I continued to broadcast as if the game were really happening. I talked about the players, what was going on, and past stats.

I skipped ahead to the end and the play that lost us the game. But instead of being disappointed, I broadcast it the way Charley had.

"I heard your broadcast the other night!" Syed said when I finished.

"Me too," Mateo added. "It was great!"

"It was pretty awesome," I said, and couldn't help but gloat a little. It *was* cool to have been able to broadcast the game. "I'd thought I was going to shadow Mosk, but he had me sit next to him and call the plays with him."

"My dad mentioned how good you were," Syed said.

"Really?" I said. People had been talking about me?

"Don't forget that she did some of it alone," Ruby reminded the class.

"Yep, as in without Mosk even helping," Myka added.

I could always count on the Invincible Girls to have my back.

I grinned, full of pride at my friends' kind words, but also embarrassed. I hadn't expected everyone to be so into this, but it was cool to see them interested instead of doubting me.

"What was it like in the booth? I've always wanted to go in there," Brady said.

"It's top secret," I told him, and laughed. Brady was basically me a few days before, thinking that everything in the booth was magical and secretive. I decided I wouldn't tell the class that inside the booth was actually boring. It was the voices at the microphone that made it so special.

"Lauren, this is one of the most interesting shadowing experiences I've ever seen. You had an incredible opportunity, and I love the creative way you presented everything," Miss Taylor said. "What are the positives and negatives of that job?"

I thought for a second.

"The hardest part about broadcasting is that you only get a break during commercials. Otherwise, you have to keep talking, or it will be dead air. But the pro is that if you know a lot about the sport and the players, it's easy to do. And as the Timber Wolves' number one fan, I didn't have trouble with that. In fact, Charley wants me to go back and broadcast our next home game with him!"

I let that sink in for a moment with the class. I didn't think anyone else had gotten asked to shadow again.

"You are the luckiest person ever!" Brady said.

"Oh, luck had nothing to do with it," I said. "What I have is talent." I turned back to Miss Taylor. "So to answer your question, the positive was proving to everyone that it doesn't matter who you are or what your age is. Anyone can succeed if they know their stuff!"

"I couldn't agree more," Miss Taylor said.

PITCH-PERFECT

It had been three weeks since we'd challenged the boys for control of the field.

Three weeks of practices and preparation.

And now today was the day. The big game had arrived, and the boys could not sit still.

"I don't know what's gotten into you, but I hope you'll be able to get this energy out at recess," Miss Taylor commented. "And I certainly hope to see you in an equally good mood when you return and it's time to start our math work."

"Oh, we will be. Don't you worry," Brady said, and while I wanted to tell him to dream on, I didn't.

None of us did.

That was step one of the brilliant plan Ruby had come up with. She called it Operation Psych-Out and claimed it was guaranteed to knock the boys off their game.

The girls agreed not to talk that morning unless Miss Taylor directly asked us something. We were dead quiet, and the boys hated it. It made them nervous. It was perfect.

We had our game faces on and planned to do whatever we could to intimidate the boys.

That was why even though I wanted to say something to Brady, I didn't. Because sometimes what isn't said is the best comeback.

Step two happened at lunch.

Or more specifically, on the way to lunch. That was when we pulled on the shirts that Emelyn had designed. They were mint green, and across the front they said THIS GIRL IS INVINCIBLE in glitter lettering, with stars over the *i*'s instead of dots. The shirts were spectacular, if I do say so myself, and when we sat down at our lunch tables with them on, from the way other kids stared, you could tell they thought so too.

"Uniforms?" Nelson shouted to us from where he sat. "When did we decide that?"

"*We* didn't decide anything. The girls wanted to remind you of who you're up against," Ruby said.

"Whatever. We don't need fancy shirts to help us win," Nelson muttered, and then bit into his sandwich.

I exchanged quick glances with the rest of the girls, and we tried to keep our giggles inside. Our plan was going perfectly.

The lunchroom monitor, Ms. Wamelink, came up to our table with a box.

"I have a special delivery for Lauren Connors," she said. "And by the label on it, I'd say it's the best kind of delivery."

"Um, that's me," I told her.

"Perfect, here you go!" Ms. Wamelink said as she set the box on the table.

"What in the world?" I said as I pulled the box toward me. "This is from Sprinkle & Shine."

"Open it!" Ruby said, and reached over to pick at the tape that held the box shut.

I swiped Ruby's hand away and ran my own finger under the tape, breaking the seal.

Emelyn gasped when I opened the box, and my stomach rumbled in excitement. Inside were at least three dozen mini cupcakes. And the letters to spell "INVINCIBLE GIRLS" were written on some of them.

"Check out the message on the inside of the box," Ruby said.

I recognized Uncle Patrick's loopy lettering on the lid. *Good luck, and be the invincible girls you were born to be! I'm cheering for you! Love, Uncle Patrick.*

"You officially have the best uncle ever," Myka said as she stared at the cupcakes.

"These are perfect!" I said. "We can share them at the pregame huddle."

Ruby reached out, and before anyone could stop her, grabbed a cupcake. "Or right now. There is no way they'll last until the huddle."

"You make a very valid point," I said, and pushed the box into the middle of the table. I called over the girls at the other tables and gestured at everyone to help themselves. None of us needed to be told twice. A ton of hands reached into the box, and we chowed down. I decided to make an amendment and add step two and a half to Operation Psych-Out. . . . Sugar everyone up before they go out onto the field.

There was nothing but crumbs left when Ms. Wamelink dismissed us.

"It's time!" Myka yelled, and now there was

no being quiet with our game faces on. Step three was full-on motivation mode. Around me the girls jumped and cheered. The whole group of us became a mint blur running toward the kickball field in a flurry of shouts and cheers.

This was it.

There was no more training, practicing, or planning.

Whatever happened out there would determine who had control of the field.

Myka ran up alongside me. "Do you think Serena Williams, Gabby Douglas, and Abby Wambach ever feel this nervous?"

I thought for a moment. "Probably before a big game or meet. It would be impossible not to feel nervous sometimes."

"They're good at not showing it," Myka said.

"So are we!" I said.

"This is it. The moment we've prepared for," Ruby said, giving an impromptu speech to the group. "We make a great team, and if we remember that and focus on how well we work together, I think we can make this happen. So, what do you say? Are you ready?"

Ruby paused, and we cheered.

"That's what I thought!" she said, and pumped her fist in the air.

"Let's get out there and show them what we're made of!" I added.

We strutted toward the outfield as if we owned it, which, when the game was over, I hoped we would.

As we played, it was like that first day when the girls had claimed the field from the boys. The game was a competition, but it didn't feel like that. We kicked, ran, and caught the ball as a team, the team we had spent all that time turning into. We cheered and high-fived when someone did something great, and told people it was okay if they missed a throw or kicked a ball into the air for an easy catch.

Here was the best part. . . . I got so caught up

in having a good time that I didn't even know the score until Ruby yelled it to the group. I didn't even *care* what the score was.

What I did know was that we were having a blast.

Carter was right. It was different when you played without thinking about winners and losers. A different that was better.

It wasn't until the very last inning that things got serious.

"This is it!" Myka said. "The score is tied, and we've got two girls on base with no outs!"

"Our time has come!" Ruby added. "Our chance to come out on top."

"Or on the bottom," Nelson shot back, but I caught a flash of fear in his eyes.

I'd like to think it was because I was up next.

I walked to the plate and stared down Mateo, who held the ball, preparing to pitch to me.

I wasn't scared.

I was ready.

The boys shifted from side to side as they waited for the pitch. They didn't know whether to move backward or forward, which was exactly how I wanted them to be.

"Come on, Lauren! Bring the girls home! Win the game for us!" Ruby yelled.

But it wasn't my game to win. It was *our* game. We had done it together, and I planned to make sure that we won it together.

I caught Myka's eye. She stood on third, bouncing on the balls of her feet.

Be prepared to run, I mouthed, and she gave me a thumbs-up.

I nodded to Mateo that I was ready for the pitch.

He drew his hand back, and when the ball reached me, I kicked it low and short. Right back to him.

I took my time getting to the base.

I wanted Mateo to know they could throw me out, that I was an easy target.

And it worked.

Mateo tossed the ball to Syed at first, and once he did, Myka jumped off third like a racehorse let out of the gate. She ran with her head down, pumping her arms, and her legs kicking up dust behind her. She ran all the way home!

We had won!

The field was ours!

All the girls ran to the center of the field and formed a big circle. We jumped and cheered and celebrated having done what many had thought was impossible.

The feeling the win gave me was such a rush. It washed over me and made me feel as if I could do anything.

"We did it!" Ruby cried.

"That was amazing!" Tyra said.

Our celebration was so loud and so full of happiness that we didn't notice the boys' reaction.

At least, not until I stepped out of the group and turned toward them. They were together in the field. But unlike us, there was no victory circle, no smiling or celebration.

The excitement from the win leaked out of me.

We were the winners.

But the boys were the losers.

And I knew there was nothing worse than losing something you cared about.

I shifted my focus back to the girls and their victory party.

I clapped my hands together to get their attention. They froze and turned to me.

"We did it!" I said, which brought another cheer out of the girls, but I held my hand up to silence them. "But now what?"

"We get the field," Tyra said, confused by my question.

"We do, but the boys lose it," I said. "And that doesn't seem right. We *all* had fun playing *together*. This started because we wanted to show the boys that girls can play kickball too."

"Which we did!" Myka said, her eyes still bright from winning the game for us.

"Maybe that's enough," I said.

"What do you mean?" Emelyn asked.

"It stunk when they told me I couldn't play with them. And now we're doing the same thing. It doesn't seem like something an Invincible Girl would do."

"So what do we do?" Ruby asked.

"We welcome everyone. If you want to play, come join the group. If not, no worries, because the field is open to anyone at any time."

"I like that idea," Emelyn said, and the others nodded.

"It's a win for everyone," Rhiannon agreed.

"Exactly," I said.

"Do you think they'll go for it?" Ruby asked.

"I sure hope so," I said. "There's only one way to find out."

I gestured at the boys to come over, and made a silent wish that they would like the idea. I'd really had a great time playing with them and would hate for that to end.

"We *all* played a great game today," I told them, "which is why I have a proposition to make."

"A propo- what?" Brady asked.

"Proposition," I said, using a word Ruby had taught me a few weeks before. "An idea I'd like you to think about."

"And what would that be?" Mateo asked, not convinced.

"We share the field," I announced. I waved my hand toward the field and then back at us. "I don't know about you, but we had a blast today. I loved playing together, and it seemed as if you did too."

Brady agreed. "It was cool to have more people to cover the outfield. And you're not that bad."

"Not that bad?" I said, and raised an eyebrow. "We scored the first run and went on to win the game."

"You're good," Nelson said, admitting what Brady wouldn't. "Especially Myka. She can place that ball wherever she wants it."

"I can, can't I?" Myka said, unable to keep the pride out of her voice.

"So, what do you say? Are you okay with sharing the field?" I asked.

"As long as I get Myka on my team," Nelson said.

"I think that can be arranged! We would be unstoppable together!" Myka said, and high-fived Nelson.

Happiness bubbled up inside me. "I officially call this competition over and declare that the field belongs to everyone. If you agree, make it known!"

The group let out a giant cheer, and with that, it was decided. We would share the field and

play together! It was a perfect ending to a perfect game!

"I would say that the Invincible Girls Club is on a winning streak," Ruby said as we walked back to class.

"We're undefeated!" Myka declared, and that was the greatest victory ever!

 # Hello, Amazing Reader!

If you've hung with the Invincible Girls Club before, welcome back! If this is your first time meeting Lauren, Myka, Ruby, and Emelyn, I'm glad to see you here!

The four of them are so passionate about making a difference, and I hope they inspire you to want to create change in your school, community, or the world!

Because remember, you're never too young to make an impact.

I especially like this book because Lauren doesn't back down from a challenge and let others define her. She tries something new and finds out that she's pretty good at it. And with her friends supporting her, how could that not be a win for everyone?

Not only does she discover her talents, but she shows those around her that girls can do anything and that a person's gender doesn't limit their abilities.

Remember, we *all* have the potential to change the world.

We *all* have the ability to do great things, big and small.

We can *all* be invincible.

So, if you haven't joined the club yet, let me extend an official invitation to come together and show the world what the Invincible Girls Club can do! We are only as strong as the woman next to us, so come, let's stand together and make some change!

Love,

Rachele Alpine

aka . . . a lifetime member of the Invincible Girls Club!

MEET
INVINCIBLE GIRL
Lindsey Vonn

Lindsey is an Alpine skier who holds the world record for the most women's World Cup race victories. She has also competed in four Olympic Games and won three medals, including a gold! When Lindsey was in the 2006 Olympic Games, she fell and had a serious injury. She had to be flown off the mountain in a helicopter. However, she didn't let this injury stop her from competing. Two days later she was back on the mountain. Lindsey is an Invincible Girl because she has never let anything stop her from doing what she loves, and she is one of the highest-ranking skiers, among both women and men, in the world!

MEET
INVINCIBLE GIRL
Serena Williams

Serena Williams is a force to be reckoned with on the tennis court. Her parents taught Serena and her sister Venus to play tennis when they were young. Their talent was soon recognized, and the family moved from California to Florida so the girls could train with a professional coach.

The two girls quickly grew in talent and are now among the most well-known names in the world of tennis. Serena has won four Olympic gold medals and is one of the top female tennis players of all time. She has even played against her sister in numerous tennis matches. Serena is an Invincible Girl because when she's playing against her sister, she roots for Venus.

MEET
INVINCIBLE GIRL
Simone Biles

Simone is a gymnastics superstar. She's won over thirty medals from the Olympics and World Championships—more world medals than any other US athlete—and she has won more world *gold* medals than any other gymnast. There is even a flip dismount called "the Biles," which is a move she developed! Simone is very close to her family and faith, and understands that her love of her sport isn't always about winning. When the pressure of competing became too much, she pulled out of the 2021 Olympics. She knew that she didn't mentally have the focus to compete, and she wanted to give her teammates the opportunity to shine. She cheered for them from the sidelines while advocating for the well-being of athletes. Simone is an Invincible Girl because she is an amazing athlete and a true team player who encourages everyone to make the very best decision for themselves.

MEET
INVINCIBLE GIRL
Katie Sowers

Katie has loved football her entire life. In fact, she has a diary entry that she wrote when she was young, all about playing football, that says, *I hope, someday, I will be on a real football team.* Katie has said that she spent much of her early life believing that wasn't possible, until she finally got her chance to play for West Michigan Mayhem, which was part of the Women's Football Alliance. She later became an assistant coach with the all-male San Francisco 49ers. And not just any coach, but the first female coach to go with a team to the Super Bowl. Katie is an Invincible Girl because she continues to work for equality in the field of football and is chasing her goal of being a head coach in the National Football League one day.

MEET
INVINCIBLE GIRL
Loretta Claiborne

Loretta is an award-winning athlete, a global speaker, and a member of the Special Olympics board of directors. As a world-class runner, she has completed twenty-six marathons and has twice placed among the top one hundred women in the Boston Marathon. She has participated in the Special Olympics World Games six times and has won ten medals, including six gold. She also has a black belt in karate and continues to stay active by trying new sports. Loretta was born intellectually challenged and with a visual impairment, so she didn't walk or talk until she was four. Loretta Claiborne is an Invincible Girl because she never let her disabilities stop her from pursuing her dreams of being an accomplished athlete.

MEET
INVINCIBLE GIRL
Katie Ledecky

Katie is a swimmer who has wowed the world with her speed. She has broken fourteen world records for women in swimming and has been named *Swimming World*'s women's Swimmer of the Year five times! She continues to train for future competitions and also gives back to the community. Swimming isn't all Katie does; she enjoys connecting with youth swim programs and talking to kids, and she received a psychology degree from Stanford. Katie is an Invincible Girl because of her speed and her dedication to the sport of swimming.

MEET
INVINCIBLE GIRL
Misty Copeland

Misty is a principal dancer with American Ballet Theatre. She didn't start to dance until she was thirteen, when her middle school drill team coach noticed her talent. However, when she did start to dance, her gift was evident. She was dancing professionally within a year! She became the first

Black woman to ever be a principal dancer for American Ballet Theatre and has been the lead in multiple shows, such as *The Nutcracker, Romeo and Juliet,* and *Swan Lake.* In 2014 President Obama even appointed her to the President's Council on Sports, Fitness & Nutrition! Misty is passionate about mentoring boys and girls and giving back to her community. Misty is an Invincible Girl because she's changing the face of dance and making it accessible to all.

MEET
INVINCIBLE GIRL
Michelle Kwan

Michelle Kwan is the most decorated US figure skater in history, having won more medals than any other US figure skater. She competed in two Olympic Games and was voted the US Olympic Committee SportsWoman of the Year in 2003. After retiring from skating, Michelle earned a master's degree in international relations. She was appointed by Barack Obama to the President's Council on Sports, Fitness & Nutrition and has worked with Hillary Clinton and Joe Biden on their presidential campaigns. Michelle also supports the Special Olympics, attending their events and advocating for those with intellectual disabilities. Michelle is an Invincible Girl because she has used her success on the ice to help her make the world a better place off the ice.

MEET
INVINCIBLE GIRL
Bethany Hamilton

Bethany is a pro surfer who lost her left arm in a shark attack at the age of thirteen. However, rather than letting that stop her, she had a special surfboard made for her and was back in the water only a month later. Then, only a few months after that, she was competing again. Since the attack, she has placed in the top three of numerous surfing competitions and travels as a speaker about facing adversity. Bethany is an Invincible Girl because she didn't let anything stop her from doing what she loved. She overcame her fear and obstacles and got right back into the water.

MEET
INVINCIBLE GIRL
Billie Jean King

Billie Jean King is a tennis star and huge advocate for gender equality, specifically in sports. Perhaps one of her greatest contributions to the world of sports was the Battle of the Sexes. Tennis player Bobby Riggs would talk about how women were inferior to men on the tennis court, and he challenged Billie Jean to a match. The match was watched by an estimated ninety million people all over the world, and everyone got to see Billie Jean beat Bobby, proving that women were as good as, if not better than, men on the court. Billie Jean King is an Invincible Girl because she challenged gender stereotypes and showed the world how awesome women are.

MEET
INVINCIBLE GIRL
Zahra Nemati

Zahra is the first Iranian woman to have won gold either in the Paralympics or in the Olympics. She was injured in a car accident, which left her paralyzed. Instead of letting that stop her, Zahra focused on archery and was part of the Iranian Paralympics team. She has also won numerous awards competing against archers who don't have physical disabilities. Zahra is an Invincible Girl because she proves that anything is possible if you put your mind to it and believe in yourself.

MEET
INVINCIBLE GIRL
Megan Rapinoe

Megan is a US soccer player who has helped lead her teams to numerous victories, including winning gold in the Olympics and winning the FIFA World Cup multiple times. Megan has spoken out about the fact that male soccer players earn more money than female soccer players, and she has fought for equal pay. She is also an advocate for the LGBTQ community and social justice. She once said, "When we, as a nation, put our minds to something, when we truly choose to care about something, change always happens." Megan is an Invincible Girl because she believes in teamwork not only on the field but also as a nation.

Ways That You Can Be an Invincible Girl and Help Change the World with Sports!

⭐ Play a game for fun; don't keep score.

⭐ Start your own sports night. Invite family or friends to join you, and create your own giant plate of kitchen-sink nachos!

⭐ Walk for a cause. See what local walks are happening around you and help raise money for a charity.

⭐ Create a donation drive for used sports equipment. Donate these items to a school, youth program, or organization that works with those who might not be able to afford their own equipment.

⭐ Volunteer to help coach a team.

★ Make signs to cheer on a local team. Hang these signs around the community or where the team plays.

★ Try a new sport (and invite a friend to join you!).

★ Adopt a field—pick up litter and clean an open area near you so that others can use it to play sports.

★ Volunteer with the Special Olympics.

★ Make or bake a snack for a team to fuel up with during a game or practice.

★ Support teams that might not get a lot of spectators. Grab a group of friends, go to a game, and help fill the stands with cheering fans.

★ Volunteer at a sporting event.

★ Create spirit packs (bags full of things like encouraging messages, snacks, and other items in team colors) to support your favorite community team.

★ Write an article for your school paper that features athletes who might not get much attention.

⭐ Hold a Silly Olympics with your friends: play fun games that will leave everyone laughing, and create your own medals to pass out at the end.

⭐ Recognize players for their efforts, not just their performance.

⭐ Attend a dance recital or performance. (Some people don't view dance as a sport, but once you see the work and strength involved, you'll agree that dancers are indeed athletes!)

⭐ Create mini first-aid kits to provide to teams or athletes.

⭐ Create your own Invincible Girls shirts and wear them proudly.

⭐ Write a letter to an athlete who inspires you and tell them you're a fan.

⭐ Start a habit to stay physically active, doing one thing each day that gets you moving.

⭐ Have your own day of team-building activities with friends, family, classmates, or a team that you're on.

⭐ Play on a team that has members of different ages, genders, and ability levels.

⭐ Hold a family game night. Challenge your family members to participate in an event where there can be some friendly competition.

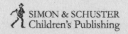

Solve each problem with the smartest third-grade inventor!

Don't miss the Mindy Kim series!

ALADDIN | SIMON & SCHUSTER, NEW YORK

EBOOK EDITIONS ALSO AVAILABLE

Break out your sleeping bag and best pajamas. . . . You're invited!

Sleepover Squad

 Collect them all!

New mystery. New suspense. New danger.

NANCY DREW DIARIES

BY CAROLYN KEENE

NANCYDREW.COM

EBOOK EDITIONS ALSO AVAILABLE

Aladdin | simonandschuster.com/kids

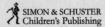